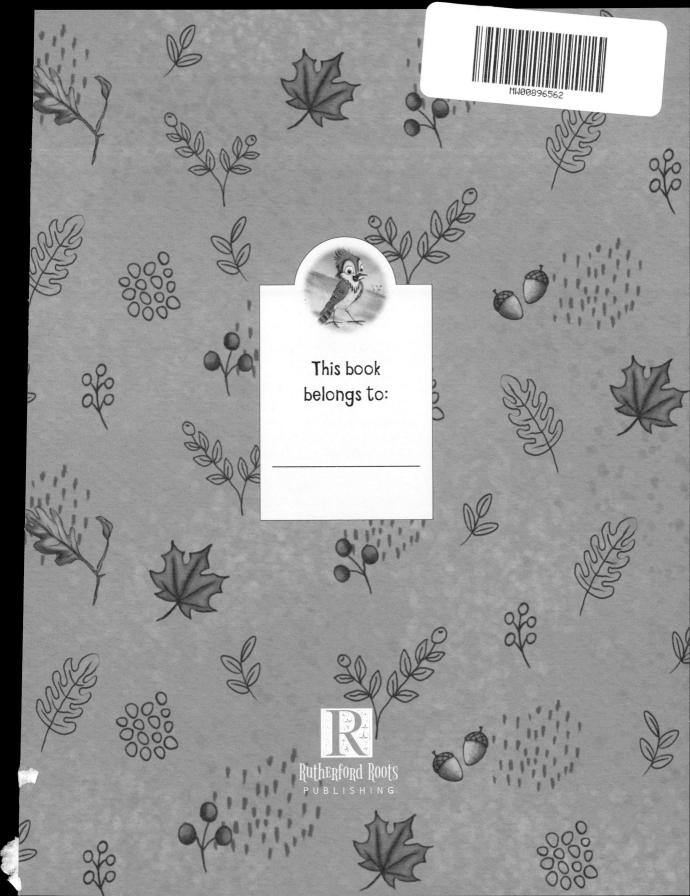

This book
belongs to:

_____

R

Rutherford Roots
PUBLISHING

To Lance and Reid, my constant reminders that the biggest
emotions often come from the smallest hearts. —DL

For all the young dreamers learning to navigate their big feelings, this
book is a reminder that it's okay to feel, and even the biggest emotions can
be gently guided with patience and courage. May these illustrations
open doors to new worlds for all who turn the pages. —LI

To request permissions, contact the publisher at publishing@rutherfordroots.com

Hardcover: 979-8-9903973-2-3
Paperback: 979-8-9903973-0-9
Ebook: 979-8-9903973-1-6

First paperback edition September 2024

Written by Darryl Lindsay
Illustrated by Laraib Irshad
Edited by Brooke Vitale

www.darryl-lindsay.com

www.rutherfordroots.com

Rutherford Roots
PUBLISHING

(Not) Ready for Winter

A Journey from Anxiety to Inner Strength

Written by
Darryl Lindsay

Illustrated by
Laraib Irshad

High in the trees,
Simon bounces around,
with eyes peeled for acorns
that fall to the ground.

He gathers and hides
every nut that he can—
to store food for winter
is Simon's big plan.

He hears some friends playing down under his tree,
and Simon shouts, "Here I come! Wait up for me!"
The fall is the time to relax and to play.
He'll gather up all the nuts some other day!

He leaps and then hops as he joins in the fun.

They giggle and laugh in the warm autumn sun.

The best time of year is before the big freeze,

when leaves tumble down in the afternoon breeze.

A soft, chilly wind whispers, "Winter is near,"
but Simon's too busy. He doesn't quite hear.

Then one day he feels the cold sneak through the air.
He thinks, *Brrr . . . I hope there's still time to prepare!*

The sunset comes sooner,
and flakes start to fall.
They're coming down quickly—
there's no time to stall.

He needs to find food
for the cold days ahead,
but patches of snow
are beginning to spread!

The cold makes him shiver. His paws won't stay steady.
It can't be that winter's here . . . I am not ready!
He should have kept gathering nuts near his nest.
The snow has now buried them. Simon is stressed!

He waited too long. Now his mind fills with worries.
He's all on his own and can't see through the flurries.

The sky turns to black once the daylight is gone.
He's scared, and he just wants to hide until dawn.

His heartbeat is racing. His thoughts are now, too.
I feel so confused! I don't know what to do.
I cannot stop shaking. My chest feels so tight.
I can't catch my breath, and I just don't feel right.

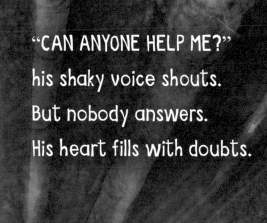

"CAN ANYONE HELP ME?"
his shaky voice shouts.
But nobody answers.
His heart fills with doubts.

He lets out a sigh
as the tears fill his eyes.
He wants to give up,
so he curls up and cries.

But up in the trees is a blue-feathered bird.

When he called out for help,
could it be that she heard?

"Come quick, wise friend Ollie!" she says. "Follow me!
A friend needs your help over there by the tree!"

"He wants to give up,
and he's all on his own.
We have to go help!
We can't leave him alone."

A calm voice tells Simon, "There's no need to hide.
I'm right here to help you. I'll stay by your side.
Remember, when nothing is going your way,
sometimes the word 'help' is all you have to say."

"You're feeling anxiety, doubts, and some fear.
Those feelings are powerful when they draw near.
I know that you're nervous. That's okay to feel.
Your feelings are one way you know that you're real."

"Just close your eyes, Simon. Try counting to ten.
Now take a deep breath, and try counting again.
Then name three things near you that you hear and see,
and move your paw, tail, and whiskers for me."

"I'm still feeling scared. I don't think I'll get through.
I gathered some acorns, but far, far too few.
I'll never find more. Will you find them for me?
They're deep in the snow, and it's too dark to see!"

"Those feelings you have cannot hurt you, my friend.
I know they are scary, but soon they will end.
Keeping you safe is a thing I can do,
but searching for acorns must be done by you."

"When everything feels like it's falling apart,
there's courage inside of your strong, beating heart.
With claws shaped like shovels and your sense of smell,
you're built to find acorns. You do it so well!"

Then Simon breathes deep, wiping tears from his eyes.
He pulls himself upright, and . . . what a surprise!
The snow has stopped falling, the clouds pass him by,
the sun rises up, and it brightens the sky!

"The snow will return, Simon. What is your choice?"
"I choose to be strong," says his brave little voice.

His tiny paws dig in the snow-covered ground
where nuts are all buried. They wait to be found.
As he carries each acorn up into his tree,
Simon learns "strong" is a thing he can be!

His confidence grows
as he gathers them fast!
He soon has enough,
so all winter, they'll last.

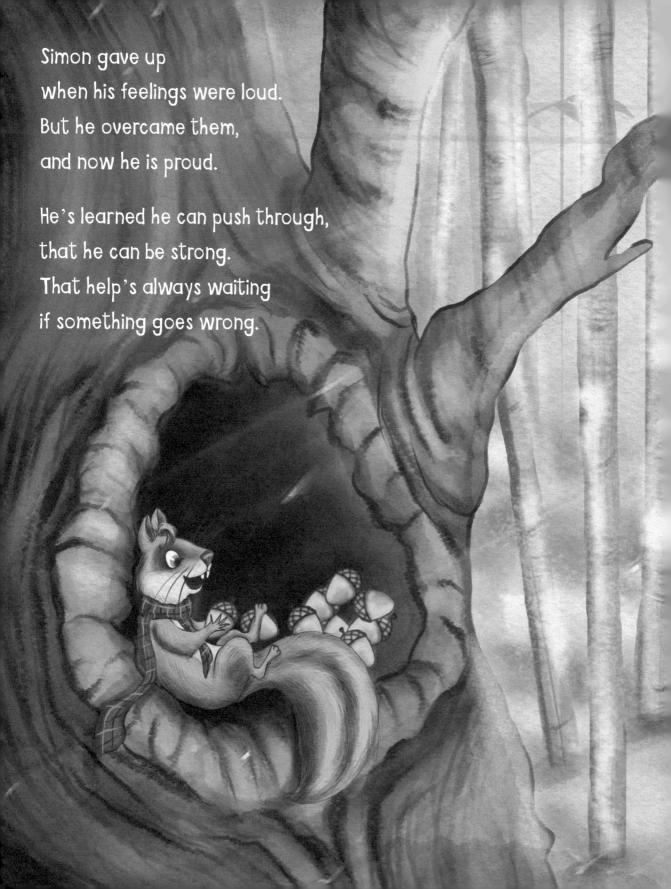

Simon gave up
when his feelings were loud.
But he overcame them,
and now he is proud.

He's learned he can push through,
that he can be strong.
That help's always waiting
if something goes wrong.

Now cuddled up warm
with an acorn in hand,

he's ready for winter
to hit the woodland.

Made in the USA
Columbia, SC
20 September 2024

42725429R00018